Be Nice, Swiper!

Written by Christine Ricci
Illustrated by Dave Aikins and Victoria Miller

©2007 Viacom International Inc. All Rights Reserved.
Nickelodeon, Nick Jr., Dora the Explorer and all related titles, logos
and characters are trademarks of Viacom International Inc.

This publication may not be reproduced in whole or in part by
any means whatsoever without written permission from

Louis Weber, C.E.O.
Publications International, Ltd.
7373 North Cicero Avenue, Lincolnwo
Ground Floor, 59 Gloucester Place,

Customer Service: 1-800-595-8484 or custom

www.pilbooks.com

Permission is never granted for comm

Manufactured in Chin

p i kids is a registered trademark of Publications International, Ltd.

8 7 6 5 4 3 2 1

ISBN-13: 978-1-4127-8925-7
ISBN-10: 1-4127-8925-7

publications international, ltd.

Once upon a time, Dora was walking through the forest when she saw Swiper swipe the Dragon's blue bouncy ball and toss it into the forest. Suddenly, the Dragon appeared, and she didn't look happy!

The Dragon was angry that Swiper had swiped her favorite ball and she cast a magic spell that turned Swiper into a banana. "The only way to break the spell is to learn the Golden Rule," said the Dragon.

"Oh Dora," cried Swiper. "You've got to help me learn the Golden Rule or else I'll be a banana forever!"

Dora agreed to help Swiper. "Let's check Map to find out where to go to learn the Golden Rule," said Dora.

Map peeked out of Backpack's side pocket. "The Cloud Prince knows the Golden Rule.

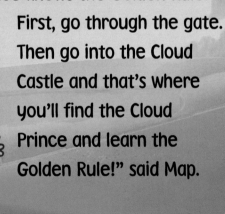

First, go through the gate. Then go into the Cloud Castle and that's where you'll find the Cloud Prince and learn the Golden Rule!" said Map.

Dora and Swiper arrived at the gate, but the gate was locked. Swiper grabbed the gate's handle and tugged so hard that he fell backwards and bumped into a little tree. "Oh mannn!" grumbled Swiper.

"If you bump into someone you should apologize," Dora explained.

"Oh!" said Swiper. "I'm sorry, tree. I didn't mean to bump into you."

The tree smiled.

"Swiper, your apology made the tree feel better," said Dora. "And look!"

A golden key had magically appeared on one of the tree's branches. It was the key to the gate.

"Thanks, tree," said Swiper.

"¡Gracias!" called Dora as she quickly unlocked the gate.

Once through the gate, Dora and Swiper saw the Cloud Castle high in the sky. "Oh mann! How are we ever going to get all the way up there?" wondered Swiper.

"I have an idea! Look!" said Dora as she pointed toward Benny floating through the sky in his hot air balloon.

"If you ask nicely, maybe Benny can give us a ride," suggested Dora.

Swiper thought about the nice way to ask for a favor and then finally he said, "Benny, may we have a ride in your balloon?"

"Sure," replied Benny. "Because you asked so nicely. Hop in."

Dora helped Swiper into the balloon and they sailed up to the Cloud Castle.

Dora introduced Swiper to the Cloud Prince. Swiper told the Cloud Prince that he needed to know the Golden Rule so he could break the Dragon's spell. "The Golden Rule is to be polite and always do what is right!" said the prince.

"Swiper," said Dora, "when you do something wrong, the right thing to do is apologize. If you apologize to the Dragon, the spell will be broken!"

Dora and Swiper hurried back to the Dragon's cave.

Suddenly, the Dragon
opened the door. The
Dragon didn't look happy.

"Swiper, I know that you can do it,"
whispered Dora. Swiper gathered all his
courage, stood up tall, and looked directly
into the Dragon's eyes.

"I'm sorry I took your ball," he said. "I should have asked before taking something that didn't belong to me." The Dragon smiled and with a poof, the spell was broken and Swiper was a fox again.

"I'm proud of you, Swiper," said Dora. "Today you learned to be polite. And even when it was hard, you did what was right."

"Yeah," said Swiper. "But there's just one thing I still need to say." Then Swiper turned to Dora. "Dora, thanks for helping me today!"

"You're welcome," said Dora. "We did it...together!"